THE TROUBLE WITH PARENTS

DIANNE BATES

ILLUSTRATED BY GUS GORDON

Supa
DOOPERS

sundance

For information regarding permission, write to:
Sundance Publishing
234 Taylor Street
Littleton, MA   01460

Published by
Sundance Publishing
234 Taylor Street
Littleton, MA   01460

Copyright © text Dianne Bates
Copyright © illustrations Gus Gordon
Project commissioned and managed by
Lorraine Bambrough-Kelly, The Writer's Style
Cover and text design by Marta White

First published 1996 by
Addison Wesley Longman Australia Pty Limited
95 Coventry Street
South Melbourne 3205 Australia
Exclusive United States Distribution: Sundance Publishing

ISBN 0-7608-0774-4

Printed In Canada

Contents

CHAPTER ONE

Everyone Else Is Coming!   5

CHAPTER TWO

"Sorry, Kids"   11

CHAPTER THREE

Aunts and Uncles   19

CHAPTER FOUR

Friends and Neighbors   25

CHAPTER FIVE

Still No Luck   31

CHAPTER SIX

Sarah's Dark Mood   39

CHAPTER SEVEN

Look Who's Here!   47

for Sebastian Viney

Everyone Else Is Coming!

"Is there anyone who won't have visitors at our Open House on Monday?" Miss Baynton looked around her class.

"My mother'll come," said Karen in the front row.

"So will my mom. And my dad," shouted Robert.

"I'll have Mom, Dad, my baby sister, Sue, and even my dog, Blackie," called Miles who hated to be outdone.

Soon everyone was calling out.

Lenka's grandmother could come. So could her mother. Sally's older brother could come.

Both of Andrew's grandparents would be there. And so would Spiro's.

"We'll run out of space!" said Miss Baynton with a laugh.

At the back of the room, Sarah and Craig looke
glum. When Miss Baynton first suggested Oper
House, they were excited. It was to be the
highlight of their class's year.

Sarah and Craig had paintings and clay models in the art exhibition. Both were in the folk-dancing presentation. Craig's project about dinosaurs would be displayed. And Sarah had been chosen to make a welcome speech for the visitors.

The twins knew that even though Open House was special, their parents would probably not attend.

Mom and Dad worked very hard, saving for a deposit on their own home. Dad was out till all hours with his carpet-laying business. Mom worked in the old people's home. She did a lot of overtime.

"We could still ask," Sarah whispered to her brother. "They might say yes."

"I bet they don't," Craig replied.

CHAPTER TWO

"Sorry, Kids"

It was Saturday before the twins were able to ask. Dad had been out all morning taking a quote for laying carpet in a new home. And Mom had been busy catching up with the week's housework.

"We're sorry kids,' said Mom. "But you know how things are. Both your father and I have to work on Monday."

"But *everyone's* got someone coming," Sarah said. "Even Benny Yerkins from the Children's Home. His social worker will be there."

Mr. and Mrs. Morgan exchanged looks.

"Sorry dear," Mr. Morgan said to his wife. "But I've got to get an order from the warehouse on Monday. And I won't be back before five."

"Well," said Mom. "We really can't afford it. But I'll ask my boss if I can have a few hours off to come to your Open House. Okay?"

That afternoon, Sarah went with her mother to the Home to help serve dinner. Ms. Sneller agreed to give Mom time off.

But later, when Mom was serving dinner to Miss Emily and her sister Miss Jessica, Miss Emily reminded Mom of an appointment.

"You're to take me to see the optometrist on Monday morning. Did you remember?" Miss Emily asked.

"Oh dear," said Sarah's mother. "I'd forgotten. I'm afraid I've made other plans. I'll ask Ms. Sneller if someone else can take you."

Sadly, Ms. Sneller had no one else to spare.

"Can't you go to the optometrist another day, Miss Emily?' Sarah asked rather crossly.

"Oh no, my dear," Miss Emily replied. "The appointment's been made for weeks. We can't change it."

Sarah wondered why Miss Emily couldn't go by herself. Or with Miss Jessica. But she didn't say anything aloud.

"Silly old bat," she muttered under her breath.

Craig was just as cross when Sarah told him the bad news. "We'll be the only ones without anyone there," he growled. "It's just not fair!"

"We've got other relatives," Sarah said, heading for the phone.

GRRRR

CHAPTER THREE

Aunts and Uncles

Sarah's first call was to her favorite aunt.
Aunty Rose was delighted to hear from her niece.
But when she heard what Sarah wanted,
she sighed.

"Oh dear, I work the day shift at the hospital
Monday."

"What about Uncle George?" asked Sarah.

Uncle George was a pilot. He was away on a trip
and wouldn't be back till later in the week.

Next, Sarah tried Aunty Lyn and Uncle Peter.
Uncle Peter had his own cabinet-making business
and worked from home. And Aunty Lyn didn't
go out to work either. Surely they would be able
to come.

Uncle Peter answered the phone. "I'd love to
come, but I've just hired a new apprentice and I
have to keep an eye on him."

"May I speak to Aunty Lyn, then?" Sarah asked.

"What's that?" Aunty Lyn's voice boomed. "Open House? No, it's Bowling Day. The championships."

Sarah was confused. "I don't know what she's going on about," she whispered to her brother.

Craig took the receiver.

"She's playing in her club's bowling championships on Monday," he told his sister as he hung up.

"That means we've failed," said Sarah. "I'll have to make a welcoming speech to everyone else's family but ours."

"I feel like an orphan," said Craig.

"Me too," his twin added.

CHAPTER FOUR

Friends and Neighbors

Craig was all for giving up. But Sarah was determined.

"Miss Baynton said we could invite neighbors and friends," she said. "So that's what I'm going to do."

Dark storm clouds were brewing when Sarah and Craig set out next day. First they tried their next-door neighbor, Mrs. Butler. They rang the bell.

A rustling came from inside the house.
Then the door rattled open. Mrs. Butler's pale
face peered through the crack.

"It's us, Sarah and Craig from next door."
Sarah spoke loudly because Mrs Butler was
hard-of-hearing.

"I've got the flu." Mrs. Butler sniffled.
"The doctor says I should be in bed."

Calling out get-wells, Sarah and Craig
set off again.

t was not easy. Mr. and Mrs. Bonacina, in the
house on the other side of theirs, both worked.
And so did Mr. and Mrs. Randolph from across
the road. Mrs. Singh said she might be able to
come. But her baby, Sandeep, was teething, and
she had to take him to the doctor's in the
morning.

"Let's give up!" said Craig, who was eager to go home to watch a football game on TV.

"You can," said Sarah. "But I'm not."

Reluctantly, Craig went with her.
"Just for another half-an-hour," he said.

CHAPTER FIVE

Still No Luck

ogether the twins tried their friends on the next
treet. It was Sunday, so some people were away
or the day. Mr. Gardiner who lived next door to
ie butcher's said he was expecting a visit from
is grown-up daughter.

George and Maria at the corner grocery couldn't promise to come either. "Too many customers. We're busy people, just the same as your mama and papa," Maria said.

George gave them an apple each to soothe their hurt feelings, but it didn't help much.

By then it was raining. Sarah and Craig splashed home through sheets of water.

Mrs. Morgan was not pleased with her two drenched and sulky children. "When you've had your baths and eaten your lunch, you can settle down with something quiet," she said. "I'm going to take a nap."

Thunder crashed and lightning lit up the sky as Sarah worked all afternoon on her speech. She didn't feel very cheerful so it was difficult to do.

She wrote the first sentence, then read it aloud. "Family, friends, boys and girls, today is a special day."

With a swift, angry movement, Sarah screwed up the page and hurled it across the room.

The next day was not going to be special. It was going to be dreadful. The others would make fun of them because none of their family and friends would be there. No one would clap especially for her and Craig when they danced. No one would praise her flower painting. Or her clay dragon with pink and mauve stripes. Or her coil bowl. No one would say how good her speech was.

Even when she went to bed that night,
Sarah was in a bad mood, her face dark
like storm clouds.

CHAPTER SIX

Sarah's Dark Mood

'I'm not going to school," Sarah announced the next morning.

'Are you sick?" Craig asked.

'I can't face Miss Baynton and the rest of the class," Sarah said.

Craig told her she was being ridiculous.

So did her mother. "Get yourself dressed, young lady. We all have jobs to do in this world. And yours is to get a good education."

Sarah stalked off to school feeling mutinous. She splashed in puddles and muddied her dress. She didn't care. Not one little bit.

The classroom was a hive of activity.
Children bunched together, talking excitedly.
Others were helping Miss Baynton decorate
the walls.

Sarah decided to help so that she wouldn't have to answer questions about who was coming to see her work. She climbed onto a desk to pin the WELCOME banner across the back of the room. The sign looked cheerful. Not at all how she felt.

Craig didn't seem one bit worried about not having visitors. He was chatting with a group of boys who were admiring the artwork.

Andrew Thompson held up Sarah's coil bowl and said something smart about its shape. It *was* rather lopsided. But it annoyed Sarah that Andrew said something.

And she was angry with Craig when
he laughed at what Andrew said.

CHAPTER SEVEN

Look Who's Here!

By recess the room was ready. Sarah went by herself to a corner in the playground. She didn't feel like talking to anyone. But then the bell rang, and she had to go back to class.

A crowd of visitors was gathered at the door.

"There's my social worker!" exclaimed Benny Yerkins.

"My brother's here," said Sally. "And he's brought his girlfriend."

Miles' family had arrived. Miles' dog Blackie had come too, just as he said it would. It charged into the classroom, barking.

Andrew and Spiro's grandfathers caught him.

Soon the class was seated. Sarah kept her eyes down. She didn't want anyone to see she was upset.

"Did you see my mother?" Karen whispered across the aisle. Sarah pretended not to hear.

Miss Baynton was directing visitors into the room.

"Hey, Sarah," said Craig, pulling his sister's arm. "There's Mrs. Singh and her baby!"

Sarah looked up. Mrs. Singh was sitting in the front of the room, rocking Sandeep in her arms. She smiled at Sarah and Craig. Sarah felt grateful. She grinned back.

Another face smiled at her. It was Maria from the corner grocery! And who should be standing next to her, but Mr. Gardiner from the house near the butcher's. And look, he had his daughter with him!

Sarah's heart swelled. Maybe Mom and Dad couldn't come. But at least she and Craig had visitors. Five of them. (That's if you counted Sandeep who was fast asleep.)

"Sarah Morgan will now make a speech of welcome," Miss Baynton said.

As Sarah was walking to the front of the room, Aunty Lyn and Uncle Peter arrived. "They called the bowling championship off. Because of the rain," said Aunty Lyn.

"And my apprentice didn't come to work,"
said Uncle Peter.

Now there were seven visitors for her and Craig.

Sarah felt nervous. Perhaps she would forget the words of her speech!

"Take a big breath of air," Miss Baynton whispered.

Sarah did as she was told. She was just about to say, "Family, friends, boys and girls," when new visitors arrived. Two old ladies slowly hobbled in. One was wearing glasses. It was Miss Emily. And the other old lady was Miss Jessica. Behind them was . . .

"Mom!" exclaimed Sarah, grinning from ear-to-ear.

"We can't stay long," Mom said.

Everyone said Sarah's speech was welcoming.
And that she had delivered it with much
enthusiasm. Red-faced with pleasure, Sarah took
her visitors to look at her artwork.

Craig came up behind them. "Look who else is here!" he said.

It was Aunty Rose. "I came as soon as I could."

"We must have had more visitors than anyone in our whole class," Sarah boasted to Craig.

Indeed, when family and friends had gone and the class counted, the twins did have the most visitors. Eleven of them. (Though Sandeep didn't really count. He'd slept through everything, even the folk-dancing!)

It had been a perfect day.

"To think I almost stayed home!" Sarah said.

Dianne Bates

Dianne Bates has written more than 40 books for children. As a child she was always in trouble for having her nose stuck in books (mostly those written by Enid Blyton) because she should have been working on her family's poultry farm.

As well as being an author, Di has worked at many other jobs. She has been a social worker in a home for delinquent girls, a factory worker, a bookseller, a teacher, an advertising sales' representative, a journalist, a TV and radio presenter, a dishwasher, and a nurse's assistant.

Di works in schools as a performer, but she also enjoys volunteer work as a welfare counselor.

Gus Gordon

Gus Gordon is a freelance cartoonist and illustrator based in Sydney.

He grew up in Northern New South Wales, and after leaving school worked on cattle stations in far north Queensland, the Northern Territory, and South Australia. Continually drawing, he left agricultural college to become a cartoonist. He has drawn for a variety of publications since; including *Australian Business Monthly* (ABM), *Reader's Digest*, and *Woman's Day*. This is his first children's book.